JACK & HIS FRIENDS WOULD LIKE TO
`DEDICATE` THIS BOOK
TO ALL THE CHILDREN —EVEN-THO—
THEY ARE VERY SLEEPY—WANT TO HEAR
...JUST ONE MORE STORY.

1

Legend written in rhyme by: Dr. David Haun
Cover Graphics & Illustrations by: Curtis Iverson

My Mom calls me Jack, and this story is told
of how I came home with an egg made of gold.

The story begins on a bright sunny day.

I finished my chores and went outside to play.

I had a pet squirrel that I loved and named Pearl.
No one I knew had made friends with a squirrel.

Both Pearl and I wandered the woods on a walk,
And Pearl found some beans underneath a beanstalk.

We brought the beans home
So that Mother could see,

And both of us planted them, my Pearl and me.
Then Pearl and I carefully watered each day

And faithfully guarded to keep pests away.

We watched and protected that beanstalk so small,

And soon with our care it began to grow tall!
It stretched, and it twisted and strained for the sky,
And it grew 'til it reached half a hundred miles high.

I once bravely climbed up a very tall wall,

But I was afraid to climb something this tall.

I reached for a limb and began to ascend,
But as I stepped up, the limb started to bend.
I jumped to the ground, and I'm telling you true;
I almost decided my climbing was through.

But I kept on thinking of climbing that plant,
Flip-flopping in thought, "Yes I can!" "No I can't!"

Then lifting my foot, reaching up with my hand,
With Pearl on my shoulder, I proved that I can.
I started to climb, scared to death; it is true.
I kept shouting loudly, "Yes! This I can do!"

Then, all of a sudden, we popped through a cloud.
Our climbing had ended. I really was proud.

Just guess what we saw, so amazingly grand –
A beautiful, wonderful, fantastic land!
There were flowers and bird nests in tall-standing trees;
I wished that **the plants** on our farm looked like these.

As Pearl and I walked, we saw fish in a stream...
Bunnies and butterflies; it all seemed a dream.

We found it so friendly, not once did we fear.
I smiled and told Pearl, "I'm glad we are here."

As I glanced to the side, I suddenly spied
A mulberry tree with a neat nest nearby.

And, there on that nest made of straw, soft and loose
Sat a beautiful, full-feathered, yellow-billed goose.

She seemed to be friendly and let me come near.
I took a step closer to see what was here.
I saw in the straw nestled under her wing
An absolute, wonderful, marvelous thing!

It looked like she smiled as she shifted her leg
Just so I could see it – a beautiful egg!

I don't know what made me feel suddenly bold;
I reached out to touch it and found it was gold!

I could have stayed with her. She liked me, I know.
There was so much to see, and I just had to go.

So, Pearl and I wandered the woods for a time
While I kept on wishing that egg could be mine.

We came to a house with a door high and wide;

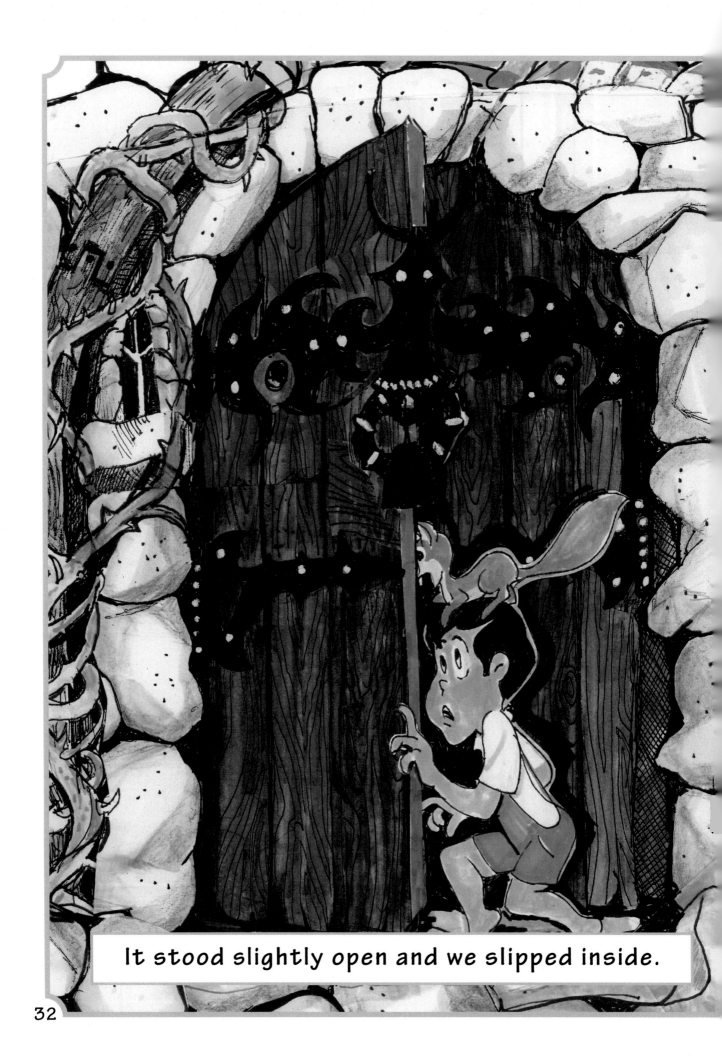

It stood slightly open and we slipped inside.

Each item was massive! I saw straight ahead
A big monstrous quilt on a great monstrous bed.
On that quilt were great eyeballs which spun around free,
Then turned all together and stared right at me.

Poking out from that quilt was a gigantic nose.
I stared for a moment; my heart nearly froze.
I felt the room shake from a humongous roar,
And knew I was hearing a humongous snore!

We tried to leave softly; it didn't work out.
Pearl upset a lampstand and I heard a shout!
"Who are YOU?" a fierce voice bellowed out with a roar,

And suddenly two ugly feet hit the floor!
I flew through that door, and I'll tell you what's more,

My feet barely touched on that green forest floor.

We ran for the beanstalk not too far away.

Screamed the giant, "I'll eat you for dinner today!"

He ran up behind me,

hot breath on my ear,

But he tripped on a tree root and flopped on his rear.

He bounced to his feet, tried to stop at the ledge,

But, he took a tough tumble and fell off the edge.

I heard his last scream as he dropped out of sight,

My knees got all shaky; I fell to the ground.
I think I passed out, but Pearl brought me around.

We walked slowly back to the mulberry tree
And the beautiful goose that was waiting for me.

She looked at me gently and honked, saying, "Hi."

I sat down beside her – lay back with a sigh.

Both Pearl and I slept. I awoke with a moan;
I lay there just thinking – I want to go home.

I spoke to the goose, said, "I'd sure like to stay,

But I miss my mother. I'll go home today."

The goose slowly stood as she stretched out her neck,
And I watched her performing a marvelous trick.

She scooped up the egg to her back with clear love
And folded her wings to protect like a glove.

Then, carefully turning, she started to walk
Down the path from her nest leading to my beanstalk.

The trip was quite straining

as we climbed back down.

Mama goose held her egg; I held her tight around.

We came to our farm

with Pearl, goose and the gold –

The first of a hundred gold eggs that we sold.

We built a new home and replanted our land,

THE HOUSE OF THE GOLDEN EGGS

A beautiful farm that was lovely and grand!

My story has ended; I wish it were true.
If it were, I'd share one of my gold eggs with you!

I hope you like our story. Please share your feelings with others. Go to Amazon.com to the book listings. In the "Review" section, enter the stars we earned and share your reaction to our book. Let them know that your special little one likes it, too. I'd love to hear from you. Email me at: writerdavid81@yahoo.com

Thank you,
David

I NEED A NAP . . .

REMEMBER US ? . . .

. . . FIND US IN <u>YOUR</u> BOOK

THIS BOOK BELONGS TO...

_____

_____

THIS BOOK WAS GIVEN TO ME BY MY.

_____, _____

I WAS ____ YEARS OLD IN _____

AND I LIVED IN _____

WITH _____

Acknowledgments

I've always loved to write and often said, "One day I'm going to write a book." We moved to a retirement community, and I joined a village group known as "Silver Scribers." The group was led by Marty Lee, a man with a lifetime of writing, photography and graphic design experience. His expertise offered a way I might write my "dream" book, and his enthusiasm excited me to try.

So, I started writing. I met another new resident, Curtis Iverson, an artist and illustrator, who had worked with Hallmark Greeting Cards and as Art Director for the Avon Corporation.

Many people, both within John Knox and outside, have helped bring Jack to life. My family, Twylah, Debbie, and Nicki, have been instrumental in the book's direction.

I could never mention the many others who have helped, but I give them all my deepest thanks. Those with a special involvement with Jack:

- Curtis Iverson
  - Marty Lee
    - Carol Redd, Editor
      - Herschell & Margo Lewis
        - Donna & Paul Westcott, Ottographics
          - South Florida Word Weavers Christian Writers Group
          - Members of the John Knox Village Rotary Club
          - The Staff and Leadership of John Knox Village and so many John Knox Village residents and friends in the larger community who offered encouragement as the book progressed. Most of all I thank God, who inspired me with the ideas, led me to people who could help, and instilled within me the drive to keep going in the process of developing a book. I've learned from Jack, the star of the book, that a person is never too old or too young to dream, think and create. I hope Jack's journey will be as exciting to read to your children as it was for us to bring it to life.

– Dr. David L. Haun

A special note to parents and grandparents
Remind your children that Jack and Pearl are make-believe. Real squirrels can bite.

"There is no greater agony than bearing an untold story inside you."
– Maya Angelou, *"I Know Why the Caged Bird Sings"*

John Knox Village
"Where possibility plays"
A premier Life Plan Community and an excellent place to live and grow
www.johnknoxvillage.com

Color Me "Happy"

Color Me "Safe"

HOME OF JACK & HIS MOTHER

Here is a page for YOU to draw and color.

Made in the USA
Columbia, SC
21 April 2019